marrow magazine

the primordial issue

AF436400

marrow magazine

the primordial issue

summer 2023

EDITORS

Elle Fournier
Kori Hensell
Jaclyn Wilmoth
Caitlin Woolley

FORMAT/LAYOUT

Kris Farmen

WRITERS

Amelia Bird
Heather Ezell
Elle Fournier
Gus Johnson
Kori Hensell
Jennifer Popa
Caitlin Scarano
H Warren
Jaclyn Wilmoth
Caitlin Woolley

WEBSITE

marrowmagazine.com

credits

"Animals I've Freed" was published in *How He Loved the Bones,* 2021.

"B Reactor" was first published in *Lime Hawk,* 2017.

"A Child A Separate Mouth" was published in *Binded,* 2023.

"Feet back in Flood Water" was first published in *Fireside: Modern Legends and Lore,* 2022.

"The Makings of a Mertailor" was first published in *The Southern Review,* Spring 2009.

"Teeth" was first published in Issue 2 Volume 1 of *Blue River Review,* 2018.

contents

Animals I've Freed

by Caitlin Scarano

The gray horse that circled the house, I've given her
oats and honey. I've undone the word starve from her
body, pushed her scapulas and ribs back
below the surface. I've forgiven myself for what I could never
understand about you, that winter. I've removed her
halter. I'm seeing her off.

The white dog we found on the tracks, nearly
blind and deaf, the one that would not come to me
in the rain. I've let go of her silence—it was an answer.
The October dark only unbroken
by the swing of headlights. I've forgiven how you
hesitated in the truck.

The baby we made in the depths of the woodstove,
I released its hand. I let it walk so far
into the forest, its body became lichen, became salal,
became cedar. I still see him on the edge of the yard,
at the edge of day. I still see him in the blue hour
you cannot fathom. Those wolves
we heard but could not find, I'm admitting defeat
to their absence. And to your absence
I acknowledge now, finally, how it made me
strong.

Bitten

by Heather Ezell

Most claim it only happens out east so let's say I'm bit when I'm five during a family trip to West Virginia. I imagine the red bullseye that swells small on my right hip. My parents never notice it because it's difficult to travel with four kids. This is why I'm in the hospital at age seven—because the bullseye wasn't spotted and the sickness was untreated and the chronic condition has led to the development of spherocytosis. It's a hereditary blood disorder but I'm the first in my family with the diagnosis.

Another option is this: It happens when I'm seven, or eight, or nine, after trekking up the brushy hillside across the street from my house. My siblings and I sit with our dad. We pass a large can of black olives around and stick the tangy fruits onto our fingertips, calling ourselves olive-hand monsters. I'm sucking an olive off my pinky when it latches onto my thigh but I don't feel it because I suck so hard I bite, the imprint of my teeth ringing my skin red. This version of events is also possible. Some say it can happen in California and my non-hereditary-hereditary blood disorder could just be an isolated fluke.

Or it could be that my boyfriend passes it to me when I'm fifteen and visiting him in Colorado. We walk a river embankment that snakes through a suburb, him asking me to hold his cigarette so he can leap from rock to rock. We sit under a spare oak tree and, circled by dry milkweed, he bites sharp into my neck. It's a mindful gesture: I'm on a vampire kick. This is how he passes me the sickness, lips latched to my skin like the legs of an insect. This origin also isn't a stretch. He'd spent some time in the Midwest—I think that's far enough east—and he's strangled with his own mood disorder and general malaise. When I fly home days later, my neck is still bruised. I think my mom notices that particular bullseye but she doesn't suggest a doctor's visit. Within a year, I'll howl for help in my sleep with dreams of senseless bloody bites on my neck, my thighs, my right hip.

In all of these versions, I'm twenty-three when a holistic doctor in Newport Beach passes me a paper with a list of the symptoms:

Fatigue, restless sleep, chronic pain, phantom smells, aching joints, muscles pain or swelling in the knees, shoulders, elbows, and other large joints, decreased short-term memory or ability to concentrate, speech problems, mood disorders, speech difficulty, fibromyalgia or chronic fatigue syndrome, IBS, blood disorders, isolated chronic pain, insomnia and depression, immune system disruptions, neurological problems, chronic joint inflammation particularly of the knee, facial palsy, impaired memory, bipolar, heart rhythm irregularities, general anxiety, dizziness, over-emotional reactions—

And I say oh thank god, that all makes sense, is there a cure?

Or maybe I give it to myself when I nip at my own wrist, when I try to stuff my fist into my mouth for something to chew. There are nights I need to gnaw at my bones. I maybe shake it loose when I punch at my swollen stiff right hip, bruising the skin until I think can see the echo of a bloody ring. I twist around to look at my lower back just to see if I've been snipped at again in my sleep. I walk outside and dare them to bite me, but I've never once seen a tick.

Chew

by Gus Johnson

I bought chicken hearts today. They were cheap.
I did what you suggested, fried them in
butter with a pan full of garlic and onion,
by no means the prettiest sight to see;

however, they were, as you say, a treat—
even better served alongside bourbon
and branch. I'm sorry I called them toothsome.
I know you cannot chew for lack of teeth.

I didn't eat them with rice and salad
or smothered in BBQ sauce, and I
fully disagree with your assessment
of the flavor. Heart, an organ and a

muscle, is not sweet, or much like liver;
more like back meat, with a pleasant texture.

Teeth

by Caitlin Woolley

I once knew a girl who didn't have any teeth. She sucked on butter and drooled down her chin and swirled her tongue around her wet lips. It's too dark in this mouth, she complained. Too puckered. Too slick. Too red.

I don't know how you can eat all those cakes, she would say to us as we gorged ourselves on the soft confections our mother baked. I licked lemon icing from the corner of my mouth. Oh, but won't you try them, we pleaded. You'll like them. They get so spongy.

She watched us and the kitchen would fill with the damp sounds of our sucking and slurping, saliva dribbling down our necks. Eventually, she would have to look at something else.

But we always wished she'd eat cakes with us.

The rest of us ate nothing else. Well, and oats, for nutrition, or sometimes other soft things, like macerated fruit or melty cheeses. The girl would eat these, too, but never the cakes. They were too sweet for her, and she said she would be sweetless.

We could not persuade her. She would not let herself be persuaded. She simply watched us eat cakes while we watched her sip milk from a spoon.

*

I should not say that it was unusual, that the girl had no teeth. None of us, not one of us in this whole house, have any teeth. Except for Mother.

But that it not to say I never had teeth. I had them once. Mother took them from me when they came in. She cupped my face and pulled them out with pliers, one at a time, kissing my cheeks. You're safe with me, my mother cooed; you don't need teeth like these.

Mother kept all the teeth she pulled, plaquey bicuspids and discolored molars (her room was filled with a rotten-sweet organic smell). She gave me cake when it was all done, when my gums were safe and clean. Then I looked like all the rest of my brothers and sisters who, like me, suffered the soft hand and the rusted pliers.

Maybe you wonder why our mother took our teeth, why we lived in her house and ate her cakes and believed ourselves to be her babies. It was because we were her babies. It is difficult to explain. The forest where Mother built her house is not a forest you get lost in; but it is the place, the sweet dark place, where each of us found ourselves somehow, friendless and unwelcome.

They say that if you abandon a bundle at the edge of the long road by the thick trees, a woman comes and takes it and keeps it as if it were her own. They say she shows these bundles such interminable love. They say she does not mind their disfigurations, that she does not miss their missing bones. These babies will have everything, if only—if only they will not leave her.

She will make them all feel loved and wanted and so, so beautiful, if only they will let her.

*

I had one younger sister, and only one. She did not eat cakes. But that was not always true.

One day, my favorite brother and I were pulling weeds from our mother's garden while she was away. My favorite brother was toothless too, but he never had any teeth in the first place, so when Mother found him, she took his ear instead.

We stopped pulling weeds when we heard rustling.

A little girl in a tattered red dress stumbled into the garden, face dirty and streaked with tears. The bowls in her hair had all come undone. Her top lop twisted up into a gnarled scar, and one dark eye sat lower than the other.

"I can't find my parents," she whimpered. "Have you seen them?"

My brother and I stared at her. We could not help it. How could we? She had such a mouth, from which yellow teeth gleamed with spit.

I had never seen anything like her. Her face, her dress, her little hands, she was even smaller than me, and I am the smallest. Her coat was full of wrinkles, and her eyes were hollow and dark. She was beautiful. My brother told her so.

She stared back at our mouths.

"They made me get out of the car," she said and started to cry.

A red bow further unraveled in her hair. She pulled it free and dropped it to the ground.

My heart dropped with it, for her.

"We have cakes," I offered. "Sweet cakes."

A soft urgency darkened her face. My brother was already reaching for her hand.

We brought the girl into the house and sat her down at the head of the table. I thought she looked very pretty there, like a picture. In the kitchen, I made a tray up for her. Bowls of pudding and applesauce. And little cakes, tucked neatly into wrappers. Lemon cakes, frosted cakes, raspberry linzer, chocolate drizzle. Angel food. Red velvet. Carrot. Flourless.

When I carried the tray into the dining room, the rest of my brothers and sisters were gathered around her like a wall of skin. They offered her clean clothes and told her she was welcome here. They offered her touch. They offered her love, and in return she did not flinch at the sight of them.

I set the tray in front of her and it must have been a long time since she had eaten because she ate the cakes and puddings all up. But we were fascinated by it. We listened and watched as she chewed, licked crumbs away from her lips, sucked cake into her mouth from the space between her two front teeth. In her mouth, we heard ourselves. We all yelped with her when she bit her lip.

My breathing quickened. My blood stirred. My mouth felt wet and dry.

Bits of sugary icing stuck to her cheeks. She picked up a lemon cake, smooth and buttery yellow. Our hearts pounded as she opened her mouth to bite into it.

"Oh, do it," one of my sisters breathed. "Oh, please."

But then Mother was home, and she was wrapping the lost girl into the soft warmth of her big body, and the lost girl was crying a deep sadness into Mother's arms, and Mother said, "please, honey, tell us your name, tell us your name."

*

They say that there is a woman whose love is so great and so huge that it becomes a wound. And this wound, this strange and terrible wound—its only relief it to cut itself into someone else.

And so we could not persuade Mother to leave the lost girl her teeth. We tried, and lobbied, and ironed all the clothes, but Mother only knows one perfect kind of love.

And the lost girl—well, she stayed, anyway.

*

After her mouth was clean, that girl refused every cake we put in front of her. I kept hoping that she would take one, just one little one, and put it to her lips. I knew it wouldn't be the same. I thought I could imagine. I thought that would be good enough.

Then, one day as my little sister and I hung clothes along the line, I considered her. She was a good girl. She kept her head down. She was kind and warm and full of new love, but even though she looked at us and didn't flinch, she didn't like to look at herself.

She remembered our birthdays and made us trinkets by hand. She did what Mother asked of her, and did it well, and maybe that was good enough for her, even if she had to be sweetless.

I looked at her through the hanging linens. All of them were gray or black or white, except the red ribbons from my sister's hair. I could smell her in the silent breeze, and somehow, she still did not smell like the rest of us.

It was unfamiliar and unsettling. I only knew the endless burn of sugar in my throat. I leaned into the linens and sniffed her. If she noticed she didn't do anything but hang clothing. Then I thought: it did not matter if Mother had left my sister her teeth. It did not matter because she would have lost them to the sweetness anyway.

At least, in this house, we were not the sum of the things we lose. We were the sum of the things our mother gave back to us.

Then, something twitched at the edge of the garden. My sister and I both looked to the sound, hands full of socks and pajamas. My heart thumped, perhaps with joy. Perhaps not. I thought of the day my little sister came to us, her red dress, the rounded yellow bones of her teeth. The cakes she ate.

She stood. I stood. I kept my hands at my sides, and wondered if I should smile.

Then the bushes parted and a little baby bluebird popped through into the yard. It flexed its periwinkle wings and waddled over the ground, picking at itself, plucking worms from below its feet.

The bird opened its beak and chirped. The beak was sharp. It was toothless. I wondered if, like my sister, it was sweetless.

I started to cry.

My little sister went to the bird, gently, her gray dress swishing along the grass. The bird did not skitter off away from her, even when she stooped, even when she scooped it into her tiny palm. She held it up and stroked its blue neck, its orange chest, its tiny toothless beak. She lifted her other hand and folded the little bird into palm-sweat darkness. The bird made no sound.

"I can feel it moving," she said, pressing her palms closer. "It is so fragile."

She turned to me and, for the first time since we got her, smiled with her red mouth open.

"We are all so loved here," I say.

*

I once knew a boy who disobeyed his mother.

On a shadowy evening he slipped away from after-dinner music and stumbled out into the mouth of the forest. He tripped over roots and scraped his knees on underbrush. He tore the soft gray fabric of his pajama pants. This did not matter to him.

He had not made it very far when he felt that his mother knew he was gone.

He pushed his little legs over stones and logs and ferns. He stretched his hands out into the falling darkness to part the vegetation and bat away spider webs. He wished he could make himself go faster, but he couldn't.

His toothless gums smacked together as he ran. Like his legs, his lungs couldn't go fast enough.

But he made it all the way up the hill, to the long road at the edge of the thick trees. He knew asphalt when he saw it even though he had never seen it before.

The boy wasn't sure if he should bring himself up to the road, possibly to be exposed, so he ran across the pavement and tucked himself into the trees on the other side. It felt like a great divide, a great distance between his home and him. He waited for headlights, believing he would recognize them.

But when the headlights came, they belonged to a massive cargo truck. Its cab was raised too high for the driver to have seen the tiny boy waving weakly at the edge of the road, and its engine too loud to have heard him over the roar. The boy tried to chase the truck, but it passed, none the wiser that he had been there.

The boy went back into the trees and waited. He waited for a long time, worrying every second that he would soon be found, that he would be made to go home.

Running and worrying made the boy so tired that he fell asleep, hidden in the bushes. He dreamed of cakes and pliers and lost girls with no teeth, and when he woke, he screamed because he thought he was in his own bed.

The sun was rising by then. The sky behind it was red.

The boy's belly rumbled, so he carefully roused himself from his nest in the bushes. He walked along the edge of the road, wondering how many cars he had missed.

He didn't know which way to go, front or backwards, so he picked one and kept walking.

He heard birds he had never heard. He counted the yellow stripes that marked the middle of the road. He looked for berries and ate the ones he found. It was his instinct to worry about the purple stains on his hands, but then he remembered what he was doing.

The road was silent.

He walked until it was dark again, and slept in the bushes until it was light. He did this for days. His belly practically howled, having only berries in it. The boy missed the cakes. He thought about eating a plant, but he didn't know which ones would make him sick, and he was sure that some of them would.

On the sixth night, the little boy, faint with hunger, cried at the silence of the road. He yowled at the pavement and its carlessness, cursed the quiet. A sudden memory of lemon cake made him drool down his shirt.

And so then, when he did see headlights, the boy stumbled into the road, waving his arms, slobbering and crying and gagging. The car slammed on its brakes and swerved to avoid him. A woman got out of the driver's side and started to hurry to the boy, but she stopped when she got close enough to really see him.

"Oh, God," she said.

"Please," the boy said, offering his palms. But she had already gotten back into her car. The smell of her tires burned his nose.

The boy collapsed onto the road and he lay there, shivering. He felt so ugly.

He laid in the road and shivered and wished that he would die. He was sorry he did not say goodbye to his favorite siblings. He was sorry, sorry, sorry. But before his little heart could give out the way he wanted a new car quietly pulled up behind him and parked. Its headlights shone above him like two bright index fingers, pointing as if now they could show him the way out of the forest.

"Oh, my poor baby," his mother said as she got out of the car and gathered him up into her arms.

He cried harder now. He cried because he was hungry, and because he did not have the strength to fight her off, and because now his new sister had no teeth; but he cried, most of all, because he knew he loved his mother.

She tucked him into the backseat of the car and pulled a blanket over his tiny body. His bones and joints no longer felt stiff or sharp. He felt defeated and hideous and he would have felt hollow, too, but his mother looked at his face in the rearview mirror so much.

"We'll get you some treats, sweet boy," she said softly. He knew there would be cakes, and that she would give him as many as he wanted, of anything he wanted, even though he had wounded her.

The ride home felt warm and long and so, so slow.

Bottoms Up

by Kori Hensell

Like how, for me
this ghostie descended (*on me*
& only me & I I I,
because I am forever
absorbed in my own
own-ness, a dark womb, only
 ever mildly aware of
the seething periphery),
awash in porch light,
its brackish circlet of hair
a bright coronet
          radiating a new kind of   passion
into the retinal bathwater—
these blinding Alabama nights.

          Remedios the prodigal
        Beauty, guide me to the springs
            of the multiverse revive me
                  with lumens
              lemons & gin.

Yonder in the shadows
by two sinewy heralds, each
bracing one
of a pair of inwardly facing monkey feet,
natural as a machine,
a tide of crimson straight
to the head
I was lifted, this brutish heart
inverted,
            the way a newbie babe
            is held under

the lamp, blushing purple
to red & pop-popped
to know it is not dead,

& all I dreaded
about the contents
of my body & all
its humours
were carried away, gently,
in a flood of hops.

*(& I thought myself so grounded, so firmly & heavily planted, anchored
not to the earth, but to the space just above—the nothing? But perhaps
we were meant to stroll the seas & by some strange evil we negotiated a
paradise of salt & energy for the dirt & the thirst.)*

Lips parted, the umbilical hose
wrapped around my infant
monkey paw,
ready to embrace the light
I, the pitiful day-worn bicycle
tire, attached to the teat,
bid to chug
        chug
           chug,
ballooned & glutted,
                "…17 …18 …19"

I the so so sad & salted
slug, upturned,
was slung back into life.

& I will be weaned.
& I will suck in the ripe & flaccid air.
& I will plunge my knuckles into the soil & plead with the
silverfish.
& on that first new equinox, having been reborn, I will jeté

through a home not my own & out

into the streets littered with honeysuckle, naked & raving,
hollering down into the hollars
where my kin are slow & fast asleep (a nasty, wet pot roast-
type sleep)
with their feet tucked & stuck to the headboard,

AREN'T WE ALL OF THEM PLANTED THE WRONG
WAY?

Feet Back in Flood Water

by Jaclyn Wilmoth

Down a side street inside a soi, which was inside a soi, which probably had no real name, Bassie had come to the only speck of light in the night. She worried that she might spook the house and send it scurrying off, taking with it the only light she could see, so she stood outside the gate and stared at it. She couldn't take her eyes off the chicken legs. They were long and slender, like the drumsticks of roosters she had only seen in Thailand. But these shanks stood twice her height. The teak of these stilts was carved into intricate feathers, which were so detailed that they ruffled as the breeze blew past. The thighs tapered down into skinny calves, which were covered with scales. The claws were sunken in the black water, but Bassie was sure they were there, grasping at the ground beneath them. On top of the teak-stilt drumsticks stood a house.

Like those of the house, Bassie's feet were submerged in water. It nearly came up to the edge of her galoshes and it stank. Years of Bangkok's sewage swam around her shins and she could almost feel the water monitors and Burmese pythons wrapping around her submerged ankles. The water itself seemed darker than the night, as if it emanated blackness. The air was still dense with Bangkok's light pollution, though the city was dark and silent. Evacuated. The electricity had been out for days.

She had been sent out to get candles the day before, so her stepmother and stepsisters had spent a whole night in the dark already, stranded on the island of their home. They refused to go out in the floodwaters, preferring instead to be encased in white tiles and walls. Even before the flood, they never liked to leave. Bassie had offered to go find candles, needing the break from that house. She had not realized that most of the city was empty. She'd spent nearly twenty-four hours already knocking on doors, sloshing through the rising water, and looking for light.

It looked in some ways like a traditional Thai-style house, carved out of water-resistant teak wood and propped up where the water couldn't reach it, designed in a time when Bangkok remembered that every year the rains brought floods, and the floods were welcomed because they made the rice grow. But now, the jungle had been poured over with concrete, so that towering trees became skyscrapers and when the floods came the water just sat. Bodhi trees and strangler figs, remnants of the rainforest beneath the city, refused to give in and pushed their way up through cracks in the concrete, dripping heart-shaped leaves on the sidewalks. This house was, however, very definitely not traditional. Old-style Thai houses did not have long, too-skinny chicken legs.

Bassie sighed and shook her head, cursing her stepmother. She had no choice but to suck it up and ask for help from whoever lived in this house-ready-to-run. Ever since moving to Bangkok, Bassie felt as if she'd been living in some alternate reality that was so close to the sun that things stopped making sense. Everything was slightly blurred by the heat, so that nothing was solid. She was not sure if the place itself was scrambled or if her brain was being fried, but this breakfast was hard to swallow.

Were those bones? Bassie walked closer to the gate but hesitated to touch it. The off-white posts of the fence were arranged perfectly parallel to each other and yet they were amiss, slightly different sizes. She took a deep breath and slid the gate to the side. It rolled easily on its tracks – for about a foot. It stopped there, as if trying to deter her. She squeezed herself through the narrow opening.

The house had one window. The light glowing from inside said there must be someone home. She walked up the steps to the front door. The edges of the doorframe were pointed into fangs, as if a snake beckoned her into its belly. She reached into her pocket and fingered its contents, asking for help. Courage enough. She knocked.

"Aren't you a little old to be playing with dolls?"

Bassie had not even seen the door open, shocked as she was by the figure before her. The woman was hunched so that she nearly folded in half. Her face was so wrinkled as to be almost inhuman. Her hair was long and white, scraggly gossamer cobwebs that swept the floor. She was squat and rounded, her skirts making a small dome and Bassie wondered what she hid beneath.

"It's from my mother," Bassie replied.

"The question still stands," the old woman squinted, taking stock of Bassie. Given the decrepitude of the woman's body, Bassie was surprised that she could see her well enough to know that Bassie was a foreigner.

Bassie squinted back and scrunched her freckled nose. The old woman's eyes on her made her aware of her body. Bassie's raven hair contrasted sharply with the ashen, wiry hair of the woman who had answered her knock. She was nearly as short as the folded old woman. Bassie was the spitting image of her mother, which sometimes made her father not want to look at her. She wondered even if this was why he spent so much time away from home "on business."

"Do you have any candles?" Bassie asked.

"Hmmf." The woman turned around and shuffled back into her house, leaving the mouth of the door gaping open. Bassie hesitated. The tiny wooden doll in her pocket urged her on, and she followed into the house.

It was incredibly small and very hot. Even in November, Bangkok was steaming. And with the floodwaters below, steaming was not an exaggeration. The air seemed as if it also was flooded, so thick that Bassie felt like she was floating. On the far side of the one-room house there was a fireplace, with a fire going strong. It wasn't often that houses in Bangkok were hotter inside than it was outside. Next to the chimney stood a giant ceramic mortar and pestle. The shutters of the house were closed and there was no ventilation, and yet the woman did not sweat.

"What will you give me for it?"

"Excuse me?" Bassie replied, widening her eyes innocently and trying her sweetest Thai-style intonation. Her stepmother's errand was already more of an ordeal than she had expected, but everything in this city was like that.

"You expect me just to give you candles and fire in this situation? They are needed by everyone."

Bassie's eyes settled on the fireplace.

"You must help an old, poor woman like me. My eyes are not good. Can you sort this rice?"

Bassie tried not to give a look of incredulity. Everyone she knew in Bangkok bought pre-sorted, processed rice. It was a modern city; there weren't rice paddies downtown. Also, Bassie was sure that this woman's eyesight was just fine if she could make out Bassie's blue, foreign eyes in the darkness and know to speak English to her.

"I don't know how to do that. I really just need to get home."

"Without any light?"

The old woman had her there. Bassie imagined returning to the cold white house of her stepmother without having anything to show for her time away.

The old woman nodded toward the bin of rice. "Just take out the stones and dark grains. And then you can cook it."

"All of it?" There must have been five kilos of rice there. Bassie scanned the room for a stove. She had never cooked over a fire and she was, honestly, not good at cooking rice. When Thai people asked her if she ate rice or bread, she always answered bread without hesitating. Not that she knew how to bake bread, either. But god, was she tired of white rice.

"It's a flood," the old woman said. "Who knows when I'll be able to cook again." She dragged the giant mortar and pestle out the front door. She turned around, "Treat it gently. You have to coax it to cook, until it's soft and plump and white. Rice is a shy, young girl. You can't force her."

The woman smiled and her wrinkles softened. In the first graceful move she had made, her hips rocked through the threshold. The mouth of the door yawned slowly open then snapped shut behind her.

With the doors and windows closed, the house started to sweat. Bassie dipped her hand into the uncooked rice, listening to the rain sound it made as it fell through her fingers. She thought back to all the times her stepmother had cooked rice since they had moved to Thailand. Plain white rice. Like eating wet Styrofoam.

Bassie took the little wooden doll out of her pocket. The carving never seemed to wear. At times like this, when surrounds were confusing and unfamiliar, this small memento of her mother was comforting. She set the doll into the rice and sat on the floor. She leaned over the bin of rice and tears started to fall, collecting in the dryness of the raw rice.

"Everything's a chore," she said to the doll. "Nothing is simple here."

She had been awake already and walking through the city for more than a day. It had seemed like such a small endeavor, to find some candles, and now Bassie wondered at what the point was. Surely darkness was easier than all this. The heat of the still Bangkok night combined with the fire weighted her head so that it drooped to the side. Her eyelids were not far behind. She let the swelter win and her childhood rushed in.

She stood in the warm sun of her homeland. The day was beautiful and she was dressed like a tiny princess, but there was an uneasiness in the billowy clouds above. Her father smiled, his gentle crow's feet twinkling at the corners of his eyes. It was one of the first times he'd smiled since her mother's death.

The brightness of the sunshine washed everything white. Bassie's pink dress, the cream dress of her new stepmother, the baby blue sky, it all glowed like an overexposed photograph. The day was too bright for comfort. Perhaps her father's smile was only squinting. The flowers were all bleached.

Bassie stood alongside her two new sisters, who sparkled in diamonds and pearls, dazzling like teeth. She was afraid to look at them.

But she could not take her eyes off her father and her new stepmother. He dressed in black, calming, soothing, and basking in the sun. He winked at Bassie and spoke words that evaporated before she could hear them. Then he smiled at this new stepmother.

The frostiness of her stepmother's dress seemed to be absorbing the warmth of the sun, soaking up the summer so that the day turned brisk. Bassie's world was getting brighter and more arctic. Blazingly pallid and corpse-like. Alabaster butterflies danced in the wind like cremation ashes. Wisps of dandelions could no longer hold on to their stems in the chill. They swirled in the drafts of sunlit air like snowflakes.

Bassie looked again to her father. The warmth in his eyes, his smile seemed to harden. His face froze into a mask.

When Bassie woke, she was covered with a gentle sweat. Cinders from the fire and tendrils of steam from the freshly cooked rice fluttered around the wooden doll as the door opened. The woman burst into the room faster than anyone her age should be able to move.

Behind the woman, the hue of the sky was changing, contrasting more and more with the black water. The sun and the water rose. Just past the front gate, a pale elephant splashed through the flood, moving clumsily like a bulky, round toddler. Bassie had seen white elephants in statues and paintings, but never in person. They were sacred in Thailand, the animal that gave the Buddha's mother a lotus before he was born, and a symbol of purity and status. Traditionally, it was not allowed to put these albino elephants to work. It was said that Thai kings used to give white elephants to people they wanted to be rid of, gifting them a large animal to feed and house which they could not use for any practical purpose. It was no longer legal to have elephants in the city, but it still happened often enough. Apparently traditions and laws went out the window as the city shut down. The mahout was easy to see, dressed all in white, like a Buddhist nun or a child ready for first communion. The water was up to the knees of the elephant. Bassie's galoshes would be useless now.

As she wondered about the best way to get home, the door slid shut. The relatively cool breeze of the outside air was cut off, as was the sweet smell of jasmine mixed with sewage. It was replaced in her nostrils by burning wood. Even the closed door was a barrier stronger than the pull of her stepmother's home.

"Finished?" the woman asked, eyeing Bassie.

Bassie quickly picked up her wooden doll and shoved it in her pocket. Her face hardened as she nodded.

"More to you than meets the eye, eh, girl?" Her voice was high and scratchy. It put Bassie on edge. The woman looked younger in this light, where the shadows didn't accentuate her wrinkles.

"May I have the candles now?"

"That easily?" The woman looked at her knowingly. "You hardly did anything." She nearly smiled. Her face contorted into a moue and at the same time her features softened. She must be older than anyone Bassie had ever met. And yet, there was a beauty about her. Something enthralling and alluring. Her eyes were lined with charcoal and the way that she squinted made Bassie both uncomfortable and titillated.

The woman scooped a bit of rice into a bowl and handed it to Bassie, who cupped the bowl as if she were trying not to touch it. She hesitated. The old woman wrapped her hands around the bowl and pushed it against Bassie's belly.

"Thank you," Bassie said, her voice caught in her throat. The woman gave her no utensils. Bassie scooped a bit up into her fingers and brought them to her mouth. The woman raised an eyebrow and sighed.

Bassie was surprised at the taste of the grains as they touched her tongue. The rice tasted of the earth, of sunshine and dirt, of the wetness of paddies. It burst as she chewed it. It was ripe and fecund, pregnant with the potential of wind and rain. The silt of centuries of floods rushed over her taste buds. It was lushly chartreuse, zipping of the first shoots of life.

"Do you have a name?" Bassie asked.

"You may call me Baba."

Bassie looked back at her bowl then shyly to the woman, wondering what was happening to her. She was not sure she could endure another bite that gushed like that. But she couldn't hold herself back. The corners Baba's mouth sparkled and egged her on. The old woman put her fingers to her own lips in anticipation. Bassie took another pinch of rice. Hours passed as she ate a few morsels at a time and each one filled her mouth with the pubescent seeds of cities, the possibility of building civilizations.

After only a bit, Bassie felt full. She yawned.

"You must be feeling very sleepy after all the work you did last night, dear." Baba raised her eyebrow and moved closer, touching her wrinkled fingers to Bassie's hair. She stood taller, meeting Bassie's eyes with a questioning, inviting brow. Bassie found it difficult to look away.

"I am, but I should be getting home," Bassie blurted, trying to keep her eyes open.

Baba didn't respond, but held Bassie's gaze.

"May I have the candles now?" Bassie shifted her weight.

"You've not done enough to earn my fire yet, girl," Baba answered. "But I will give you another task."

"Another one?"

"Or I could eat you," Baba answered. She did not smile. She stroked Bassie's chin.

Bassie could hardly keep her head up. "It's so hot in here," she said.

"I need chili paste to go with the rice." Baba brought out the mortar and pestle. The mortar was large enough for a person to fit inside it and the pestle would clearly take two hands to move. Or I could eat you. Baba opened the door to a small closet, which held a store of chilies, garlic, and onions piled on the floor. Some of the onions rolled to her feet. Bassie gave the woman an annoyed look.

"Keep your sass in check, girl, and make sure you make it plenty spicy. The paste should be hot and fiery on my tongue. I'll be back." As Baba opened the door, the midday light filled the room. It was stiflingly hot. The floodwaters oozed the brackish green of sewers and rushed higher, climbing the steps to Baba's house. The air filled with the smell of Bangkok's klongs, black canals that ran past malls and corrugated metal shanty towns, soaking up everything the city excreted. Bassie couldn't stomach the idea of wading or swimming home in that.

In the daylight, she could better see the gate that surrounded Baba's. Thighbones, shins, and arm bones made the posts, while collarbones held them together lengthwise. Every few meters a skull was placed on a raised shoulder blade. The eye sockets glowed in the noontime sun, as if alive. The bones were orderly, forming an intricate embellishment which stretched all around the house. Bassie pictured Baba standing on a pile of bones, skulls in her hands, dancing a primal ritual of death and creation as she built the fence. Her arms flailed as if she had ten of them and her eyes glowed a savage red. And Bassie was alongside Baba, weaving with her a shining mandala, a protective reminder of the circle of creation and destruction, all made of human bodies.

This was too much for Bassie. She made her way slowly down the steps of Baba's house. Most of them were underwater. She went in to the top of her galoshes, realizing that there were still four more steps to go. The water was nearly up to her neck and surged, rushing quickly to the south. There was a splash at her ankles the darkish green of the water lapped at her thighs. Pushing out of the flood was a water monitor, its forked tongue licked her legs as its claws wrapped around her. Bassie ran up the stairs and back to the safety of the belly of the house, slamming the door behind her.

Inside, Bassie tentatively approached the mortar and pestle. She touched the ring of the mortar. There was something comforting about the roundness of it. The way that it curved was inviting and Bassie nestled herself into its concave cradle. And here she was, motherless, alone a hemisphere away from her birth, in the middle of a natural disaster.

She took the doll out of her pocket and gently ran her fingers over it. It was short and voluptuous, wood made soft by the hourglass contours. It was so small and round that it was barely recognizable as human-shaped and yet it echoed memories of her mother perfectly. Bassie fell asleep clutching the doll in the embrace of the mortar.

Cuddled by the warmth of her childhood home, which was cuddled by the coziness of the forest, Bassie burrowed into her mother's lap. There were fireflies all around, dancing in pairs, starry eyes keeping watch over her. Embers from the fireplace floated in the air and congregated in Bassie's hair and on her mother's chest. Her father watched them from across the room and worry wrought his face.

Her mother coughed and reached under the blanket. As the wind blew the trees outside held hands and danced in a circle around the house. Bassie wanted to join, but she wouldn't leave her mother's lap. The wind sang a song and used their small house as a drum.

"Kvass, please," her mother said.

Bassie's father hesitated before making his way to the kitchen. As he left, the fire was emboldened. Flames illuminated the room. The light frolicked on the floor, on the ceiling, on Bassie and her mother. The walls smiled. Autumn leaves looked into the window, asking to enter. They pressed their fiery faces to the glass, waiting eagerly to see what would unfold inside. The fireflies and embers pirouetted together, unsure of who was flying and who was falling.

"This is for you." Her mother opened her hand to reveal a small wooden doll. Its features were finely carved: flowing wooden hair, softly draped wooden skirt. Two of the fireflies came to land on the doll's face, setting her eyes aglow and the doll's lips parted as it sighed.

"Ask her for help when you need it, Bassie, but don't forget to feed her. She will be everything you will ever need." Her mother coughed again. The fire coddled them in its blanket. Bassie hugged the doll under her chin and fell asleep.

In Baba's house, Bassie woke next to the fire and had trouble seeing straight. The room was suffocatingly hot. Her hair stuck to her face and neck. The door was open, but Bassie was alone. The fresh air was too apprehensive to enter, so she had to track it down herself.

She sat on the front steps, an enticing snack framed by the mouth of the door, and wondered if she could coax the house into running away with her. She could sit on these steps while the chicken legs picked up and ran out of the flooded, steaming metropolis into some idyllic rainforest. She could be alone, running naked through banana trees and orchids. No stepmother, no stepsisters, no chores. Just singing mangoes and cicadas.

She thought of lost pasts and lost futures. She tried to remember when it felt like to be home. It was gone now. The house she grew up in, the land she grew up on, they were no longer hers. The people who had made her feel at home were no longer hers. Even the dreams she'd had of traveling and making homesteads in foreign lands had evaporated. She felt adrift in the floodwaters. A compass was useless because there was no direction toward which she could travel. She could not go back, nor could she move forward.

In the distance, flood waters splashed. With glazed eyes, Bassie looked in the direction of the sound, taking very little notice of the elephant and rider passing in front of the gate. The animal was a pinkish red, the color of clay. Its backside swayed and bewitched. The scarlet mahout stared at Bassie, but she was too deep in rainforest to meet the gaze.

"Finished already, eh?" Baba appeared on the steps as if out of nowhere, dry and fresh. Her hair seemed to glow in the light. Her eyes and lips looked fiery.

Bassie tried to peel her hair off her skin. She felt unkempt and self-conscious next to Baba.

"Where's the chili paste?" Baba asked.

Bassie didn't answer and Baba pushed past her into the house. Bassie followed.

The mortar held a sticky, red chili paste that stuck to the sides of the mortar as if clinging to a lover. Bassie's doll rested between the mortar and the pestle. As Bassie rushed to stuff it in her pocket, Baba raised an eyebrow.

"Give me your hands," she said.

"What?"

Baba grabbed both Bassie's hands by the wrists and lifted them to her face. She eyed them carefully and then touched Bassie's fingertips to her tongue, slowly, suspiciously. Her mouth was warm and smooth. She took one finger into her mouth and sucked.

"Clean," she said. "You haven't touched a chili."

Bassie pulled her hands away. "I used the pestle."

"To separate the tops? To cut the chilies and the onions?" Baba said. "I'm on to you, girl."

The woman scooped paste out of the mortar with her finger and touched it to her lips without opening her mouth. It turned her lips crimson and her cheeks followed suit. Her eyes gleamed as if a switch had been turned on insider her. With another scoop, she reached her fingers to Bassie's lips, applying the same fiery lipstick to Bassie's confused mouth. There was a rush of heat, from her lips to her face, and washing down through her body. Bassie licked her lips and the flames inside her seemed to make the heat of the fire-lit tropical house more bearable. Droplets of sweat traced the contours of her body and Baba followed each trail with her eyes. The heat rushed to Bassie's head and she closed her eyes as if she'd been caressed for the first time.

As Baba smiled at Bassie, she glowed that light of women who are pregnant or in love. Her hair was thick, curly and bright, flames licking around her face, illuminating her crevasses so that there were no shadows. Baba ran her fingers over Bassie's jaw line and Bassie's skin tingled.

"This will do," Baba said. Baba offered her more chili paste and she took it eagerly, hot for Baba's approval. They fed each other gently, as the sun began to set.

The fire was dwindling and the room was sticky. Rain started to beat against the roof and Baba got up to open the door, hips swaying as she went. The rains had traveled down from the Himalayas to cool Bassie's skin and left small mountains of gooseflesh on her arms. Tiny Everests poked out from beneath her shirt. Baba didn't turn to look as Bassie walked up behind her. Instead, she kept her eyes out into the night. Passing in front of the boney gate was the darkened silhouette of an elephant and its rider, moving easily and deliberately through the water, as if they had slowed to look at Baba and her hungry house.

"They pass every day," Baba said to the rain. "They always pass."

Mahout and beast continued to lumber past, softly churning the floodwaters as they moved. The city was silent and Bassie could hear the small tsunamis that the footsteps of the pachyderm sent toward the chicken-leg island where she stood. The eerie glow of millions of lights that had been turned off days ago still hung in the air, particles of light pollution held in place by the humidity, caught and magnified by rain that fell and didn't fall. The tiny light droplets backlit the mahout and the elephant, silhouetting them as one imposing, blackened animal. Bassie reached for Baba's hand and Baba returned her grasp.

"There's one more thing I want you to do for me, and then you may have my fire."

Bassie did not object and Baba led her back into the house. The sultry heat of the room rushed to envelop her, tousling her hair. The elder climbed up on a chair and reached for a sack on a high shelf. As she reached, her body unfolded, revealing breasts, hips, an hourglass waist. She threw her head and shoulders back as she grasped the sack and she looked strong, young. Bassie expected her to crinkle back into the rotund, enfeebled crone who first opened the door to her the night before, but she didn't. Bassie pulled herself straighter, trying to stand as tall as Baba, whose hair no loner touched the ground. Bassie thought she saw herself in the old woman.

Baba put the sack on the floor and opened it. Tiny black teardrops spilled out, crawling and writhing out of the bag like ants.

"Sesame seeds," Baba said, as Bassie recoiled. "Nothing more. They need to be cleaned." Baba handed her a small cloth. "One by one."

Bassie nodded and dropped to her knees. The heat in the room lulled her eyelids together as if they were lovers on a torrid night. Her head drooped. She begged not to fall asleep while Baba was at her back. She straightened her shoulders and pulled herself awake. In her pocket, the doll stirred.

Baba rested a hand in Bassie's hair. "There, there," Baba said and Bassie could hold on to wakefulness no longer.

It was a hot, obsidian night, the kind of black that glowed with the reflection of the lights around it. From inside the taxi, a young Bassie stared mesmerized and spellbound. City lights shone, from convenience stores, from motorbike headlights, from the tiny bulbs of street carts. A family of five passed on a motorcycle, baby sandwiched between parents and toddlers grasping handlebars and mother's back. A leathery woman wove orchids into wreaths and the scent shot through the windows and air conditioning of the car, smacking Bassie in the face. A man cycled past with a plastic display case instead of a little basket in front of his handlebars. As Bassie peered into the case, she saw a display of crickets, cockroaches, and beetles, all spiced and sautéed for sale. The sights and smells were cramped in, pushed up against the nudging shoulders of the taxi by the concrete walls that grew up on all sides. How could this place ever be home?

Together in the backseat with Bassie, her stepsisters slept. The metropolitan lights hung heavy in the air, blurred and refracted through the thick, tropical heat. The lights left trails behind them, as if the whole city were a nighttime photograph taken from a shaky tripod. The glares fluttered and flew in the air. The gaping mouths of her stepsisters yawned, inhaling and exhaling the night. They sucked in the glow of the street vendors and shops, swallowing Seven-Eleven signs and tiny bulbs hanging from extension cords attached to stalls. In the front seat her stepmother, face of stone and determination, seemed to push the taxi on.

As the green and yellow cab moved further down the soi, the road became narrower and more packed. There were no other cars anymore, only stalls and motorbikes, pedestrians as wide as the alley itself. The taxi nudged past all of them, none of whom noticed or acknowledged the car in the road. In front of the taxi, the city glared with the lights of commerce. Her sleeping sisters sucked them up one by one: the lights of the noodle soup stalls, headlights of motorbikes, blue TV light from inside evening homes. Her sisters' snores inhaled them all, swallowing them into the darkness of their stomachs. In the wake of their traversing was left only blackness, black eyes, black air, black street, black hair, black buildings, black stares.

When Bassie awoke, Baba was sitting next to the fire, arms crossed into a pretzel over her chest. Her skirts were pulled up to her knees, which poked out shapely and full from beneath.

"I saw the whole thing, darling."

Bassie was still pulling herself out of her dream back into Baba's chicken-thigh cabin. Baba motioned toward the shining pile of black sesame seeds. On top of the newly cleaned pile sat Bassie's most prized possession, her little wooden doll. Its eyes glowed and it quivered.

"I knew there was more to you. You are destined for greater things."

Bassie shivered and stayed quiet.

"You can always count on natural disasters to bring fate to the forefront. When the earth starts to rumble and the waters get angry it only means that something is amiss and needs to be set right. And here you are."

Baba rose from her chair. When she stood straight, Bassie admired the curve of her hips and breasts, the wave of her waist. Her hair had darkened, to a flaming black, making an ebony halo around her face. Her skin glowed so that Bassie wondered if she would be hot to the touch, and she reached out a hand to her. As she brushed her arm, she felt a buzz; static sparks radiated from the contact.

"Eat, dear. You deserve it." Baba handed Bassie a bowl full of the rice, chili paste, and sesame seeds that Bassie's doll had prepared. The flavor was more than the sum of the ingredients. The rice burst with the fertility of seeds. The chili paste burned with the zest of passion. The sesame seeds brought them together in a deep, mature richness that filled every corner of Bassie's mouth. Baba ate too and together they became giddy on the fullness of the meal. Bassie moved closer, resting her head on Baba's chest. Baba enveloped the whole of her body, as if her arms were wings enclosing around her.

"You've earned my fire," Baba told her. In an overturned skull, she placed a candle and lit it with the fire from her hearth. As the flame on the wick grew, the fireplace darkened, leaving only embers.

"It's time for us both to go home," Baba sighed. "I'm so glad you've come."

Bassie pulled away from Baba's embrace and laid herself on the wooden table behind her, inviting Baba to follow. She did. Hips and thighs and the curves of bellies, collarbones, jawbones, and spines all mixed together on the table. Bassie latched on to Baba and buried into her. She gulped all she could from Baba and Baba did the same, creating a spiraling mix of nectars through their bodies. Baba dined on toes and breasts and gasps and Bassie nibbled elbows and buttocks and sighs. They gorged and swallowed until they had their fill.

Or I could eat you.

On the pile of rice, chili paste, and sesame, the eyes of Bassie's doll glimmered like glowworms and it rattled in a way that it never had before. It seemed to have a wind about it, some intangible movement that held the air surrounding it. With the gentleness and ease with which things fall apart, it broke perfectly in two.

The hewn grandmother gave way to a seductive, passionate woman, who in turn gave way to a shy, misplaced girl. It was a doll within a doll, which broke again and again. Like the outside, the inside layers were not painted, but delicately carved. The smooth features of an array of beauties were etched into solid wood. Outwardly, she was a grandmother, large and portly, all encompassing. But within her there existed ever-smaller selves until at her core she was a mere babe. She held within her generations yet to burst forth, versions of herself yet to be fleshed out. The dolls danced past Bassie and Baba, caressing their bellies and cheeks until they fell asleep.

On the pile of limbs and flesh, the doll broke open fully. Inside was the smallest, most unbreakable piece of all, a tiny house standing on chicken legs.

When Bassie awoke, she was alone. The flame in the skull continued to burn in the corner of the room and the embers of the hearth had dimmed. The sky was just starting to fade. Bassie stood at the bottom of the steps, feet back in floodwater but this time without galoshes. The water had started to recede. In the twilight she could see the reflection of her own glow. Her hair had grown, reaching almost to the water and it was a shock of white that framed her face. She waded home, though empty streets and sois. She passed water monitors and pythons and looked them in the eye. They held her gaze and watched her march. Mango trees dropped their fruit in her hands. Even skyscrapers paid attention as she glided by.

When she reached her house, it was empty. Her stepmother and stepsisters gone, fled from the flood. She checked her room and the kitchen for some note, some forwarding address and found none. They had left her alone, far from the city of her birth, abandoned in a flood. Exhausted, she melted onto her bed and dreamed every dream she had ever known simultaneously.

She was sticky and hot, not just Bangkok hot, but something more. It was bright in her room, and smoky. The lines around her blurred and swirled and crackled. A fire raged around the skull that held her candle. She moved closer to it and it lapped at her feet. She reached for the skull and her hands cupped the flames, comforted, warmed. She brought the skull out of the house and stood in the waters. Turtles and river crabs came to sit beside her. She watched until the sky started to glow and splashing noises behind her pulled her out of her trance. A mahout rode a white elephant past and Bassie wondered if it was the same one from the start of her journey. The mahout had hips that swayed with the elephant's stride.

She was dressed in white cotton gauze, like a Buddhist nun, but the cuffs of her sleeves and pants were trimmed with silver beads. They tinkled as the rider passed. Her face and head were covered with the flowing cotton. She nodded to Bassie and a lock of glowing black hair fell from her headscarf.

Bassie knew she had only one place to go, and that it would be empty when she got there. She took her still-lit skull and started the procession back to where she'd been. The door of the house gaped open wide, inviting her inside. The snake mouth seemed to smile as she entered. Baba was gone and Bassie knew she would not be back. The rooster legs of the house twitched, ready to take Bassie anywhere she pleased. Her matryoshka doll sat on the mantle, whole and sealed shut. Its eyes glowed like embers of a fire from within its belly. She was home.

42

B Reactor

by Elle Fournier

The site was chosen because of its isolation and because of the abundance of water from the Columbia River, which could be used as a coolant for the reactor...B Reactor produced plutonium that was used in a test explosion at White Sands, New Mexico, and in the bomb dropped on Nagasaki.

-Zach Cook, Nuclear Legacy

The sun falls behind our mountain
like a child colors an Easter egg;
he splatters red and yellow vinegar
on mother's favorite dress,

leaves only silica to sparkle.
When we were smaller
we thought it might be uranium
glittering in the sand—

or tips of spider legs, still with life
left to grasp our bombing-range soil,
weaving threads of talc
between private underground pools,

snagging the 60,000 apparitions
that dangle from delicate spools.
Beneath paltry abundance,
a spindly swingset under desert noon,

every morning we dug, raw-handed
and Fruity Pebble fresh, scooping down
until the sand was wet and cool.
Once, we dug so low we stood

tip-toed, bottom-stranded—
waiting to hear mother whisper
in father's ear; the muffled
cry of airplanes we counted two

by two; the murmurs of a patient

monsoon. No one had told us
what the water knew—
how to weave graveyards

into rope ladder,
to press pursed lips
against earth, to suck away.

Plum: (adjective)
Considered Very Good or Worth Having

by Jennifer Popa

a lyric biography for Jill

The girl and her sister commit their first crime together. Plucking plums from the neighbor's tree. Plums which they did not ask permission to take. Plums purpled with sunshine. Plums who waited so long to be plucked they sometimes released their grasp on the branch, chucking themselves to the earth. A thudding sacrifice. Plums calling out to the girl who is allergic to bananas. It is a plum day for picking plums, the plums say. Who was she to ignore a plum? A plum asking to be loved by a mouth. A plum with the whole of its family looming below. The rot of their cemetery. Each folding in upon itself on a summer afternoon in Texas. On account of the neighbor's inaction, on account of the waste, the two girls pluck. Only later do they learn they are thieves.

It's no surprise the thieving child becomes a thieving adult. Only she does not steal. She simply suspects herself of guilt over her blessings. For a time love only hung around in two-week increments until one stopped liking the other. Then a man splits her life into the before and the after. She does not trust that she is her husband's favorite. Sometimes she wonders aloud why do you love me? She is insistent in the question. He is insistent that she stops asking it, insistent that she is so much. You just are, he says. She is unaccustomed to being anyone's favorite.

Someday she might have a baby, or she might not. If she does it will only be for curiosity's sake. She will not tell it that being a human is a fucking nightmare, will tell no son that we must live so long aware of our own deaths. But when the son inevitably learns this truth, she will teach him the trick of sleep. Teach him to tell himself stories in the maw of night. Never anything interesting, only dull imaginings. She will teach the child that if the brain marvels too long, insomnia invites itself in like an ugly lover on a lonely night. If the child cannot sleep, she will feed him sliced plums. Each alternating: sweet then sour. She will insist he is her favorite and it will be true. She will never worry that she will stop liking him.

A Child A Separate Mouth

by H Warren

My hands will make a tower of dead grass
and crush the ants that climb the hill before
I spit the chipped ends of my coral teeth
out for you a keepsake remember me
I will split your lips apart and sign our
palms with the blood of your tongue with my tongue
a prayer rotten bruised like apple skin
I will think about the way a fist can
bruise the bone like wine stains carpet red like
vibrations from my mouth when I'm at home
with no one else at home to hear the dog
howl moon howl hard whispers in the darkness

you ghost how I howl as you approach me

48

The Makings of a Mertailor

by Amelia Bird

1.

Strings in casings drew up the curtains. Bubbles spewed from the bases of the sills on the other side of the glass, creating an effervescence that obscured everything. A boy searched through the bubbles. He heard a tinkling sound, lower an octave, which became a sort of music accompanied by a swishy hiss. The bubbles slowed their pouring. Behind them: a mermaid, hovering in the space between the distant grotto walls of the deep blue spring. She swam toward the audience, her head up, smiling, pushing the water behind her with her fin, and scooping with her arms. Her golden tail flared at the tip. Long hair floated around her face in the raucous slow motion of underwater. She paused and angled her tail to one side. With a few fingers, she touched her mouth and blew a bubbly kiss, scattering the shiny bubbles with a sweep of her arm. They rose quaking, tiny feathers in opposite gravity.

The boy's grandmother thought to nudge him playfully at the sight of that kiss, but when she looked down at him, she saw a spell she couldn't bring herself to break. Eric sat completely still, leaning forward slightly. His feet hung limply and his eyes had grown wide. They glistened with the blue light of underwater. Something in him had shifted, a channel dug and the water diverted.

2.

Shortly after going to the mermaid show at Weeki Wachee Springs for the first time, five-year-old Eric Ducharme searched under his parents' sink for garbage bags. He found a box, pulled out a handful, and took the bags to his room along with some scissors, masking tape, and a hot-glue gun. He sat on the floor, wrapped the garbage bags around his legs, and glued the bags together. The glue took too long to dry, so he grabbed the silver tape and wound it tightly around his legs. He taped the garbage bags over his feet and shredded the bottoms. The tatters swished as he scooted across the living room floor and the kitchen tile toward the screen door that opened to the pool.

A few weeks later, after two more trips to see the mermaid turn slow, arm propelled circles while holding an air hose between her teeth, Eric's grandmother discovered him in her closet, tying one of her old, silky nightgowns around his ankles. She took him to Jo-Ann Fabrics.

The next day, yards of straight, satiny, bluish silver material covered the living room floor. Eric sat on it. He traced the shape of his legs onto the fabric. He estimated the space the fins would take, put them on, and sketched around their rubbery edges with chalk. He cut out the tail shape in double and asked his grandmother to sew it up for him. Inverted, it was his first mermaid tail. Nearly a thousand mermaid tails later, his parents and grandmother are proud of the name he has made for himself: Eric Ducharme, the Mertailor.

3.

How I fit into this has something to do with how it feels to be underwater in the rain. When I was a little girl and the lake level was high and the water clear—a combination of factors that didn't always coincide—I swam as often as I could. Most of my time in the water was spent completely submerged. I'd settle into the sandy bottom and fan upward to keep my body down. The water felt warm compared to the air. All pressure slipped away, leaving only the slight sensation of hands pushing on my eardrums. Rain droplets on the lake surface made a frosted ceiling of light. The blurry, muffled underwater silence fizzed into a high, cottony hiss, a tssssss, a light twinkling of sound. The blub of exhales turning into bubbles rose to meet the diamonds mottling the water's surface, now my ceiling.

I never learned to scuba dive, never swam competitively, never allowed my relationship with water to be anything more technical than held breath, the pills on the bottom of my hand-me-down swimsuit pressing into the sand, and the absolute quiet to be found there. The tails came when I was much older, in my twenties, but felt like an attempt to reconnect to that notion of escape—the simplicity of being an animal in a place, a feeling I swam to with a spiraling of knees and flipper.

I found Eric Ducharme when my first tail was under construction and I was tooling around the Internet looking at examples. In him, I saw another person working to extend that feeling of escape you find underwater—a person doing what I'd done as a child, but doing it on a much larger scale.

4.

Over the entrance of Weeki Wachee towers a statue: the pale white figures of two women performing an adagio. One woman balances the other in the air, a few fingers pressed to the small of her back. The woman on top arches her spine, one knee high in the sky, her arms extended, as if falling into a backbend. Her hair flows stiffly. All is perfectly poised, down to the flippers on the women's feet. In the time before the performers wore tails, the mermaids used to adopt this pose deep in the cave of the spring, drift up with the boil toward the surface.

Beneath this statue, Eric ran to the ticketing booth holding the silvery blue sack he'd sewn. He was going to swim in his homemade tail at the place where he had first seen a mermaid.

Buccaneer Bay—the water park portion of Weeki Wachee—looked then pretty much like it does today. A dock was anchored in the spring run that flowed past a wide beach of trucked-in sand dotted by umbrellas. Bright yellow water-slide chutes dumped kids with wedgies right into the spring water, water that's seventy-four degrees year round.

While little boys Eric's age dunked each other in the pale blue shallows and older boys stood on the dock or did cannonballs near the lifeguard, Eric sat on the sand of the swim area, his mermaid tail at his feet, and began inching the fabric up his legs. He had to lie back on the sand and lift his pelvis to wiggle the tail's material up and over his swim trunks. As he smoothed it over his legs and started a fin-first, caterpillar crawl toward the water, a few of the boys in the shallows doubtlessly looked over at him. They might have giggled, but Eric didn't notice. He was thinking the flippers could be more tightly bound by the tail's material. Lowering himself into the water, he noted that he could see the shapes of his kneecaps through the wet fabric. Not good enough, he thought, having barely swum at all; I'll have to make another one.

5.

Today, Eric Ducharme is one of the top mermaid-tail makers in the country, maybe the world. It's a small industry, accessible by Google search and mail order. There are a few tail-makers who are well known. They all have opinions about each other's work. Eric's one of the big ones. And he is only seventeen.

His quiet state is louder than most people's. He ticks every now and then, looks around, appears anxious. His deep and close-set blue eyes are sharp but skittish. He always needs to be doing something with his hands. Now and then, he sniffs compulsively.

I asked him, over lunch at a seafood restaurant, if he dreams about being underwater. He considered the question a long time before answering. "Probably," he finally said. "Yeah." He turned his attention back to his picked-over chicken fingers. He doesn't eat seafood.

"I'm living my dream at such a young age," he had told me earlier over the phone. "I have just always been really, really creative and driven." He continued, "Just so you know, I'm not working for Weeki anymore."

Eric had been doing what he'd waited his whole life to do: perform for Weeki Wachee, the place that had started his obsession, his business, his identity. He swam in the shows as Prince Eric, tailless, though the mermaids wore his tails. I asked how long he'd worked for Weeki.

"About six months," he replied. "But I quit last week because… well, it's like I told them all the time: how can you have mermaids without mermen? It just doesn't make any sense."

6.

Weeki Wachee is a tourist trap; Weeki Wachee is a treasure trove. Weeki Wachee: tossed up or washed up or still going strong, kitschy before anyone thought to aim for kitsch. Best known by reporters and postcard collectors, Yankees and lovers of roadside curiosities, tourists and teenaged girls. Weeki Wachee, the underwater mountainscape. Weekiwachee—one word—in Muskogee, coming from "wekiwa" and "chee." "Little Spring" or "Winding River" as named by the Seminole Indians. To the mermaids, just Weeki.

A large-magnitude spring, one hundred and twenty feet deep, Weeki Wachee pulls forth a flow strong enough to knock the mask off a snorkler, spilling the cool contents of the Floridan aquifer system into the sand hills of west peninsular Florida. The water is always warm. On cold mornings, stretch marks of fog tease the glassy surface. The spring pool is miraculously blue. In the 1930s, freshwater-spring enthusiasts claimed it to be the clearest water in the state, so clear you could drop a coin in, watch it sink a hundred feet, and witness a puff of smoke as it struck the white sand bottom. Underwater slopes harbored rare, aquatic plants with leaves that tinted red, purple, and green when they waved in the current, reverberating through the blue.

In 1947, Newt Perry, a barrel-chested man known as "The Human Fish" dove into the water to scout for a location for his dream. Looking down the blue, cavernous hole through his mask, Perry had to remind himself that one couldn't gasp underwater. After the Gulf Coast Highway was put in and a crane had hauled the old box springs and automobiles from the spring's bottom, Perry built an underwater theater the size of a boxcar, tied weights to it, and sunk it. A sign was erected, a few girls from down the road taught to breathe pressurized air and eat bananas underwater, and Weeki Wachee became one of Florida's few roadside attractions—the only thing going on for miles.

ABC bought the attraction in the 1960s and replaced the tiny, old theater with a million-dollar one that could seat five hundred people. The spring was walled in on all sides, glass tucked inside the walls to create a space for viewing, the viewing space drained, trenches dug, pipes and lines buried, and cement poured for a parking lot. Today, the spring is developed on every side, surrounded by hundreds of thousands of homes and golf courses and the neighboring Disney World, which draws a crowd the size of a major university's population every single day—competition so fierce the attraction in the spring water can barely stay afloat.

But the vision! The undiscovered world of performance in zero gravity! The canvas of the spring water filled with water nymphs who can fly! The tails didn't really get established until the 1970s, but it was always Weeki Wachee, home of the Aqua Belles, the Undines, the Aqua Maids, the Loreleis and their underwater boys, and the occasional sea turtle. Weeki Wachee, "The Only City of Live Mermaids," the mermaid center of the free world, just a few blocks from Eric's grandparents' house.

7.

The first show Eric saw performed at Weeki Wachee is the only show to be performed in the underwater theater for the last fifteen years: The Little Mermaid. He'd already seen the Disney cartoon so many times that he had it memorized. Then he saw Splash, and it became his favorite because he prefers "realistic-looking tails." All these productions share the root of Hans Christian Andersen's 1837 fairy tale. The show at Weeki Wachee, Disney's cartoon, and Splash all have happy endings, but in Hans Christian Andersen's telling of The Little Mermaid, the lovely, nubile mermaid doesn't win the prince during her time on land with legs, and the prince cannot, in the end, breathe underwater and return with her to the underwater kingdom. Instead, the mermaid spends her last days on earth absolutely miserable. She weeps all the time. Every turn of foot feels like she's stepped on a knife. Her last action on land is to perform mute, somber, I'm-about-to-die-and-turn-into-sea-foam dances for the prince and his new bride. She bleeds through her shoes. In the end, instead of simply dying, the little mermaid turns into a spirit of the air—part of neither world she has known and loved.

But all contemporary mermaid tales end happily. Ariel wins Prince Eric and a wedding is the finale. The same goes for Splash and the shows at Weeki Wachee. These stories seem to say that if you try for something purely and in earnest, it will all work out just as you wish.

8.

Eric took so quickly to Splash because the fish tail that Madison wore, the mermaid character played by Daryl Hannah, was so perfectly crafted. The tip of her wide, caudal fin shone with a ribbed transparency that eased into the vivid orange of Japanese koi. The back midline bristled with a fringy dorsal fin. Two quaint pectoral fins, like fish hands, came out from where her quadriceps were hidden. The orange scales melded into her belly skin.

During the making of the movie in the early 1980s, Thom Shouse, the foreman of the film's tail-making crew, commonly known as the "Tail Man," constructed the tail out of Plexiglas and Skinflex, a urethane compound that was new on the market and had been used primarily to make prosthetic limbs. That tail carried the screenplay and made visual the aquatic dreams of many people, not the least of whom was Hannah. The actress refused the option of a swimming double. She swam so fast in the tail that the underwater makeup artist and the three divers toting her scuba tanks had trouble keeping up with her.

Eric's initial reaction to Splash was similar to many people's reactions. Sort of a, How did they do that? The difference between Eric and most people is that his next thought was, How can I do that? He spent the next twelve years figuring it out.

9.

"I always have to have things match," he told me. "I don't know why; I just do."

In his father's garage, he squatted over a seaweed bra he had just painted the same color as his brand new, realistic tail—a tail to rival Shouse's. We were about to drive to Rainbow Springs to try out the tail with Mermaid Abby, a friend of Eric's from Weeki Wachee, but he had to heat-set the paint on the bra first. A scalding hair-dryer contraption purred in his hand.

Eric drives a blue Mustang with a chrome mermaid lounging near the taillights. When the bra was dry, we put the flippers and masks and everything in bags, and he lined the trunk of his car with thick plastic so it wouldn't get wet from the tails.

10.

Eric's grandmother gave her Kenmore sewing machine to him when he was eight years old, because, after making five tails for him, she figured it was high time he learned to sew the seams himself. Eric discovered that the zigzag stitch isn't the only option for a strong and forgiving seam. Experience with stretch fabrics taught him how to predict how many centimeters a fabric will give. He learned the hard way that materials with sequins, tiny plastic mirrors, glued-on spangles, or lines of glitter make the sewing machine shudder and the thread break. He also saw how spangles and mirrors flake off in the water—bad for the design, bad for the fish.

Eric began searching out Lycra-spandex blends. He got really into faux velvet. He ordered bathing-suit liner in bulk. He trimmed the edges of the tails' tips with scarving. He cut scuba fins to make the flippers resemble a dolphin's. He pushed his Moto-Tool drill bit through lion's-paw shells. He made casings for tubing to add structural support to the fins, creating a tail design he called "the triggerfish." He aimed his industrial heat gun at thin, vinyl strips to make them curl like kelp in a current and painted them a shimmering green, pioneering what came to be known as "the seaweed bra." He made tails that matched bra tops that matched jewelry. He began experimenting with neoprene.

11.

When he wasn't at his machine or in elementary school, Eric was at Weeki Wachee. After months of begging, he convinced his parents to let him attend "Adventures Under the Spring," Weeki Wachee's mermaid summer camp. He was the only boy.

There, he met Barbara, a former mermaid. Barbara noticed Eric's interest in the performances and got to know him because he was always at the park. As soon as he was scuba certified she offered to teach him how to breathe out of an air hose. He slept over at Barbara's house—everyone calls it "Mermaid Mansion"—on the weekends. Between shows, he and Barbara swam together. She taught him tricks in a tail. She told him, "Eric, you can be a merman if you want to," and he believed her.

The first tail Eric sold was Barbara's doing. A fashion designer, Sara Dionne, who would later coauthor a book on Weeki Wachee, had been shooting interviews for a documentary on the park's history. Sara wanted to know where she could get a few tails for a fundraiser for the film, so Barbara called Eric at his mother's house. Soon, Sara was giving the measurements of her calf's widths and inseams to nine-year-old Eric, who was trying to act professional.

Eric finished the tails with help in a little under a week. Twins Holly and Dolly, who had once worked at Weeki Wachee, wore the tails in the Coral Room, a bar in New York complete with a nine-thousand-gallon saltwater fish tank.

Eric's business was launched. He made mermaid tails for Halloween. One black with a bone design, one blood red. He made tails for the Fourth of July with fireworks on them and red and green ones for Christmas. He made tails of different sizes to keep at the pool behind Barbara's mermaid mansion. He wore a tail he made to his grandparents' fiftieth wedding anniversary. He filled two bulk orders for Weeki Wachee Springs, making fabric tails for mermaids and former mermaids, altering many because the girls had lied about their waist sizes.

He made tails with zippers and tails with dorsal fins. He received an order for a tail made of long, shaggy fur.

"I don't work with fur," he replied.

He received orders for erotic tails—tails with holes in certain places, tails that covered a person's head and shoulders—but he didn't fill those orders. He received an order for a pink tail from the principal of a high school who had lost a bet with his students over the grades they would make on the Florida Comprehensive Assessment Test. He made a tail for a star on American Idol. He made tails that were worn once for Glamour Shots, tails that never got wet. He made tails for little girls who had to be supervised when they swam near the deep end. He made tails for sexy ScubaRadio women to wear in a shark cage off the coast of Guadeloupe. By the time he was fifteen years old, the website Eric had created and maintained—www.themertailor.com—came up first in a Yahoo search for "mermaid." By the time he turned sixteen, he had sold more than six hundred tails.

12.

At the finale of The Little Mermaid show, the mermaids surface at the opening of the mermaid hole, which is the end of a sixty-foot-long submerged tube that connects the show's dressing room with the spring's cave. Eric, on the other hand, would exit the water and climb a stepladder onto the theater roof. After experiencing the silence of being underwater for nearly an hour, he would suddenly be bombarded by the sound of squawking tropical birds from the bird show, screeching kids on the water slides, and yelling parents, and by the smell of pretzels and pizza and steaming pavement. He'd pick up a white, gauze shirt and button it as he walked across the roof toward the doors for the part of the day when he carried a mermaid to the photo-op area.

He would stand to the side of the low, wooden bench next to the mermaid while the crowd poured from the theater. His job was to smile and keep out of the photographs—the same kinds of mermaid photographs he collected when he was a kid.

13.

When Eric was allowed to wear a tail at Weeki Wachee—that is, when the theater was empty—the tail he wore was a more ornate model than those the mermaids used at the time. It was deep blue velvet with silvery trails meandering along it like creeks. Diaphanous cloth hung at many angles from the tail fin, and as he moved to the beat, it followed a half step behind. The underwater speakers emitted a tinny version of the music. The treble trickled through the water to his ears.

"You want me to play the track again?" came a woman's voice over the speakers. Since the installation of an underwater sound system in the 1970s, there had been no male announcers because their voices were too low to carry through the water.

Eric looked toward the blurry wall of windows and nodded.

In a tail, there are limits to what moves you can do. No arabesques, they taught him, no side leaps, no Shinkos. Pinwheels are out and so are marlins, and definitely no adagios, and don't even think about making anything up. In tails, routines consist of back-kneed dolphins, swan dives, backflips. Straight legs in these moves, not much undulation for the family show; an arc of the spine and the arms push circles to rotate the whole body forward or back.

Eric had choreographed two routines—one set to One Republic's "Apologize" and another to Fergie's "Glamorous"—even though he only needed to show one to the mermaid manager, Marcy, to finalize his rise in the Weeki Wachee performer stratum. He'd moved from trainee to novice early on, passing the tests easily. He swam the thirty-odd feet down to the stage, took off his mask, put it back on, filled it with air by exhaling. He swam across the theater windows twice in one breath, practicing.

Eric performed in two shows a day, five days a week during the summer, and two shows a day over the weekends when school was in session. He wore a prince costume, shorts with contrived shipwreck edges cut jagged above the knees. When he wasn't doing the falling-in-love-dance with the Little Mermaid or fighting the sea witch, he got no action. He could have been ready to perform his routine for Marcy at any time, but whenever he brought it up, she insisted that he hadn't worked there long enough to make the leap from novice to merman. So instead, he tweaked his dance between shows.

During the planning of the yearly mermaid calendar, one of the mermaids suggested that Eric appear "in one of his fantastic tails." Robin, the general manager, nixed the idea. "People expect girls," she said.

"But how do you get mermaids without mermen?" Eric joked.

Eric quit before he got a chance to perform his routine for Marcy. But even if he'd been promoted to merman, he would have spent all but two days out of the year being a prince. Only one show at Weeki Wachee involves a man in a tail. In the Christmas show, the starring mermaid's father, the sea king, swims up, waves regally to the crowd, lip-synchs a few words of the recorded scene, and then disappears again into the air lock in the castle.

14.

I stayed up all night making my first mermaid tail. I riveted flippers together and sewed crooked seams. It was a fluid movement in the water I wanted, the feeling of being a different kind of creature, and some abstract notion of embodied and shareable magic. It wasn't until I tried out the tail in front of other people that I realized how naïve I had been.

I brought it to Silver Glen Springs in central Florida with some friends. There were other visitors in the spring there, too. People snorkeled or waded in the clear shallows or looked at the water from picnic tables. As soon as I wiggled into the tail on the submerged stairs and stood up to jump in, everyone in the water and on the banks looked at me. Little girls pointed. Adults looked confused, tried to look away, stared back at me again. Self-consciousness overwhelmed me. I slumped into the water and started to swim. I wanted to feel myself moving with the water, and began to, but then noticed all the masks pointing at me. All the sudden, the flippers and bathing-suit material stretched over my calves and thighs had ceased being a personal experience. I had turned myself into a spectacle.

Putting on a mermaid tail inevitably implies performance. And yet there is an inconsistency here: performance, even if inevitable, is antithetical to the point of donning the tail—to be something outside yourself and magical and in tune with spring water.

15.

I asked Eric if he went swimming with other mermaids and mermen, if they took field trips to springs together, by themselves and just for fun. He answered, "We do photo shoots with models when I finish new tail designs. They all have to be tried out."

"Do people stare at you?" I asked.

"Yeah," he said. "A lot of people don't understand why we'd want to do something like this. They act kinda confused." He went on, distantly, "I smile at people and try and be friendly and most of the time everyone's positive and excited and I'll take pictures with them and send it to them if they want. But every now and then I get weird comments when I have a tail on. People aren't used to seeing a man in a tail. But I've learned just not to care what people think. They're just jealous. If they've got a problem, it's really a problem with themselves."

Eric is cautious about revealing his sexuality, but the subtext is strong when he says something like that. His e-mails sometimes contain lines like, "My dad's friends just don't understand my world."

When I am watched underwater it is for different reasons than when people stare at him. Girls are allowed to be mermaids, objects of fantasy. When Eric puts on a tail, people assume flamboyance or that he's cross-dressing, which is not necessarily the case. Eric's "mer-world" is not an attempt to escape from his gender. Underwater may be more real to him, may allow him to be more authentic than he feels out of the water, but it is a world that still abides by rules and norms that are beyond his control.

16.

On the dock at Rainbow Springs, Eric was too cold to not look vulnerable. His jaw was penciled with a thin line of hair along his chin, and his teeth chattered cartoonishly. He clutched his chest with his arms. Goose bumps covered his shoulders. They shook.

"You don't really have much flubber to keep you warm, do you?" I said.

"I know, right? Thanks for noticing."

He was chubby as a child, but now he has the body of a well-toned swimmer. His figure is important to him: since quitting his job at Weeki, he has been trying to promote himself as a merman model. He introduces himself as "Eric

Ducharme, Mertailor and Merman Model." It is the tagline on the bottom of all his e-mails. Really, I now know, it's a way for him to stay submerged.

Rainbow Springs is the headwaters of a clear, wide river. About thirty miles from Weeki Wachee, it is another west coast, blue green jewel embedded in Florida's sand hills. One dollar each got us in to swim in the designated area with a metal dock with metal ladders. A line of buoys denied us access to the larger spring boils around the bend. Eric said he'd probably swim past the buoys and out to the main springs "because what are they gonna do?" but we stayed in the swim area the whole time, probably because he was so cold.

Abby, an ex-Weeki employee and friend of Eric's, hauled herself out of the water and onto the dock. She flung up her flipper and then stood, carefully, keeping her balance with Eric's help. Tails, out of the water, utterly restrict the wearer. Eric shivered his way over to inspect part of the tail at her waist. A mystery substance textured the surface of the neoprene and gave it a scaly relief, a sleekly aquamarine glow, and the appearance of being perpetually wet.

"You know what? That's gonna look awesome. That's not even really peeling off in the water. But with another clear coat… I'm there! It swims like one of Thom's tails!"

"It swims better, actually," Abby corrected.

"Really?" Eric said, peering closely at the surface of the tail.

Abby had worn two of Thom Shouse's tails for a photo shoot. She said of the tails that they were really hard to get on and off because the material stuck together if the surface folded in on itself, which is somewhat inevitable.

"Yeah, because I can bend my legs," Abby said. Eric looked down at the monofin flipper he had cut and adhered to the coated neoprene. With his toe, he pushed on an area that seemed to have caught a bubble of air.

"It's slightly buoyant," Abby continued. "It's kind of hard to tell since it's so shallow. But I could really pick up some speed."

Eric had also met Shouse when he came to Weeki Wachee with one of his famous tails, a model, and a photographer. He took Eric seriously after Eric asked him questions about his tail design for Splash and his more recent designs, technical questions regarding construction and material. The two formed a business friendship, communicating for months until Thom's replies dropped off.

17.

Over the phone a few weeks after our visit to Rainbow Springs, Eric was willing to talk about his decision to quit working at Weeki Wachee. In the fall he had been sick for a few days with a sinus infection—an illness prevalent among merfolk because of the water pressure—and the manager had insisted he attend practice anyway. He was to play the male part, tailless, of course, in the Halloween show.

I asked him what the days were like right after he quit.

"A sense of relief, definitely, because I could dedicate my time to my mermaid dream. A lot of times I would cry and be very upset emotionally, but more doors started to open." Calls came in from ScubaRadio. A diving convention in Orlando gave him a place to display his tails. He received tail orders from an underwater artist, scheduled an interview with a Japanese documentary film crew. He was going to start making mermaid calendars and greeting cards, trying to promote himself as a merman model.

Eric has lived his entire life in Citrus County. Often Abby suggests that when he's old enough to do such things, he ought to open up a shop in Miami or Hollywood or West Palm, someplace in Florida with a younger tourist population, somewhere more important and urban than the Gulf Coast. He shrugs politely as a reply to suggestions like this, says, "I know it's small, but I like it here."

Eric knows about every mermaid venue there is. Trying to find more outlets for sales led to a larger search for places mermaids performed, other underwater communities, so to speak. He discovered a number, but none were as grand as Weeki Wachee. The resort in the Bahamas put mermaids on inflated doughnuts in their chlorinated pool. At Aquarena, an old attraction in Texas, the underwater girls wearing ballet shoes and skirts got laid off when the theater facility closed in the 1960s. There was a place in Japan—he knew about it because an underwater performance artist named Shinko had emigrated to Weeki Wachee from there but it was basically a giant fish tank, similar to the Coral Room in New York. As for the shows in Vegas, they were scandalous, used only female performers, and took place in constructed environments replete with fake coral and types of fish that normally wouldn't hang out in the same hemisphere. Weeki Wachee is still the only place Eric knows of that uses water that isn't chlorinated or pumped through a filter, the only place where, when turtles swim by, they do so by choice.

Weeki Wachee suffered quiet beginnings. It arrived long before jet skis, preceded the hullabaloo about manatees. The Springs came into existence before there was a need for such a title as "The Nature Coast." Back in those days, in the first years the park was open and before Newt Perry had to sell it because he was unable to turn a profit, Perry would tell his mermaids to stand near the road to flag down passing cars. The girls, clad in the modest one-pieces of the time, convinced those they could that there was something back there in that spring, a phenomenon they would regret missing even though they had never dreamed such magic existed.

The spring water changed before Eric was born. In 1976, the Weeki became cloudy when a nearby conduit collapsed, spilling silt into the river that feeds into the spring. The mermaids tried performing a Sherlock Holmes show to make the most of what looked like dense London fog, but they couldn't see to do even that. For the first time since the 1940s, there were no mermaid shows for nine months. As the spring began to clear again, it filled with brown algae, dreary piles of it, and all the colorful, aquatic plants died. By the time Eric went to the mermaid show, the water wasn't drinkable anymore, wasn't as invisible as oxygen.

But tainted or not, the mystique persists: the water has never stopped offering itself in cupped hands toward the sky. How was Eric to see the springs' limitations before they held him back? Weeki Wachee was what he had, what began who he now is, and, however limited the ways of its waters and the policies of its mermaid shows might be, they haven't yet released him. Listening to Eric talk about his business successes, one would think they made up for the loss of Weeki Wachee. "I hope the management there will change," he told me. "If I could go back tomorrow I would be there."

18.

That day at Rainbow Springs, Eric scooted off the dock with a mask and his digital camera and followed Abby to deeper water. Their heads rose together above the surface. They took a synchronized breath and then descended. A minute or two passed with bubbles on the surface, then their heads rose for another breath. After taking some forty pictures of Abby in the tail and coordinated seaweed bra for the Web site, Eric returned to the dock to drop off the camera and pick up a tail for himself. By this time, a few people were walking near the dock. Eric stood and zipped the tail up the back to his waist—for this one was a zippered, pro tail—sat on the edge of the dock, then pushed off into the water. A boy ran to the edge of the dock in time to catch a glimpse of the tail underwater, waving as it moved away from him. The boy and I watched Eric join Abby in deeper water, gazed at the boil of their bubbles on the surface, their mercurial shapes.

"Pretty cool, huh?" I said to him.

He looked at me, folded in on himself with shyness, and returned to his father.

When Eric and Abby got back to the dock, out of breath, people were there waiting for them.

"Hey! Do y'all swim at, um… Wika Wachee?" a woman called from the side walk above the swim dock.

"No," Abby called to her as she struggled to stand up in the tail. "We used to."

"When did you last go to Weeki?"

"Last February."

"I was there then," Abby said.

"I wasn't yet," Eric said. "You saw my tails, but—"

"We really enjoyed it," the woman said. "That place is totally wild!" A few minutes later an older couple joined us on the dock.

"Are you from Weeki Wachee Springs?"

Eric replied robotically, "No. We used to work there."

"He designs the tails," Abby said. "He's made them for Weeki but he works on his own now."

Eric recited prices for children's tails to the people around when they asked. He described the difference between his fabric tails and his newer, realistic tails.

"What's this stuff on the surface here?" someone asked, touching the slick, scaly surface.

"That's my secret. Neoprene mostly. And other things."

At some point as we chatted with people on the dock, the little boy alongside me who'd been watching the mermaid and merman tugged at his father's shirt and asked if he could have a merman tail. His father laughed and said, "I don't think so, hon." Eric, busy answering someone else's questions, didn't notice this interaction.

contributors

Amelia Bird is a writer who lives in New Orleans.

A Southern California native, **Heather Ezell** graduated from Colorado College with a BA in English literature and creative writing. After bouncing between Washington State and Alaska for several years, she again lives in California and works as a writing instructor, book coach, editor, copywriter, and photography retoucher. Her debut novel, *NOTHING LEFT TO BURN*, was published by a young adult Penguin Random House imprint in 2018.

Elle Fournier is a writer, teacher, and PhD candidate in English Rhetoric and Composition. She grew up in the shrub steppe of Washington state.

Gus Johnson holds a creative writing MFA from the University of Alaska Fairbanks. He's currently dreaming of his own artisan barbeque sauce business.

Kori Hensell is learning how to be Florida Woman™ while fostering a poetic life. She broke her wrist at a house party while busting slippery moves to La Roux. (She/her.)

contributors

Jennifer Popa is a short story writer, essayist, and occasional poet. She earned her Ph.D. in English at Texas Tech University and did her MFA in Creative Writing at the University of Alaska Fairbanks. She now works as an Assistant Professor at Gannon University where she is revising a collection of short stories and a novel. Some of Jennifer's most recent writing can be found at *The Florida Review, Bellingham Review, Moon City Review, West Branch, Ninth Letter,* and *Sundog Lit.* She can be found at www.jenniferpopa.com.

Caitlin Scarano is a writer based in Bellingham, Washington. She holds a PhD from the University of Wisconsin-Milwaukee, an MFA from the University of Alaska Fairbanks, and an MA from Bowling Green State University. Her second full length collection of poems, *The Necessity of Wildfire*, was selected by Ada Limón as the winner of the Wren Poetry Prize and will be released in spring 2022 by Blair. Her poetry chapbook, *How He Loved the Bones,* (which this poem first appeared in) was recently released by Lillet Press. In May 2021, Bear Gallery (Fairbanks, Alaska) exhibited Caitlin and Megan Perra's collaborative project *"The Ten-Oh-Two"*—poems and visual art on the Porcupine Caribou Herd. She was selected as a participant in the NSF's Antarctic Artists & Writers Program and spent November 2018 in McMurdo Station in Antarctica. You can find her at caitlinscarano.com.

contributors

H Warren (they/them) is a poet and musician from Fairbanks, Alaska. Their work is featured in journals like *"SOUND Literary Magazine," "Water Stone Review,"* and *"Pilot Light,"* as well as the full-length album, *"Mother Carries"* by Harm. Heather is a 2019 Rasmuson Individual Artist Award recipient. Their first full-length poetry collection, *Binded*, is forthcoming with Boreal Books/Red Hen Press.

Jaclyn Wilmoth writes novels that are memoirs and memoirs that are novels, often with a sprinkling of poetry. She is the author of *The Snow Witch* and the founder of Lightning Droplets. As a child she displaced a growth plate and she hasn't grown since. Now she lives in Alaska with her writing husband, nature-loving daughter, and emotionally unavailable rescue puppy. (She/her.)

Caitlin Woolley is a Seattle-based writer with a speculative bent and a love of language. She has had 12 teeth pulled. (She/her.)

about marrow

Marrow is a literary magazine committed to publishing work that explores dark spaces. We're interested in writing that uses compelling language and imagery to remind us what it means to be human, that makes wonderful the plain and strange the ordinary. We accept poetry, fiction, non-fiction, hybrid, and multimedia pieces.

Read more at marrowmagazine.com.